Lottie Perkins

For brilliant boys and girls everywhere.
Yes, that's you! – KN

For my dear family: Ichiro, Seiko, Taro,
Takuto and Kenta – MK

 The ABC 'Wave' device is a trademark of the
Australian Broadcasting Corporation and is used
under licence by HarperCollins*Publishers* Australia.

First published in Australia in 2018
by HarperCollins*Children's Books*
a division of HarperCollins*Publishers* Australia Pty Limited
ABN 36 009 913 517
harpercollins.com.au

HarperCollins*Publishers*
Level 13, 201 Elizabeth Street, Sydney NSW 2000, Australia
Unit D1, 63 Apollo Drive, Rosedale, Auckland 0632, New Zealand
A 53, Sector 57, Noida, UP, India
1 London Bridge Street, London SE1 9GF, United Kingdom
2 Bloor Street East, 20th floor, Toronto, Ontario M4W 1A8, Canada
195 Broadway, New York NY 10007, USA

A catalogue record for this book is available
from the National Library of Australia

ISBN 978 0 7333 3905 9 (paperback)
ISBN 978 0 7333 3909 7 (library edition)

Cover and internal design by Hazel Lam, HarperCollins Design Studio
Typeset in Bembo Infant by Kirby Jones
Sticker scene and insert printed in China by RR Donnelley
Printed and bound in Australia by McPherson's Printing Group
The papers used by HarperCollins in the manufacture of this book are
a natural, recyclable product made from wood grown in sustainable
plantation forests. The fibre source and manufacturing processes meet
recognised international environmental standards, and carry certification.

Lottie Perkins

MOVIE STAR

BY KATRINA NANNESTAD
ILLUSTRATED BY MAKOTO KOJI

ABC
Books

CHAPTER 1

My name is Charlotte Perkins.

My friends call me LOTTIE.

I'm an exceptional child.

I'm good at nibbling toast into interesting shapes.

I'm good at dressing my rabbits to look like famous people.

I'm good at writing my name backwards.

I'm good at fogging up windows.

'You are an exceptional child, Lottie Perkins,' I say to myself. 'And don't let anyone tell you otherwise.'

'Charlotte Perkins, you are a DAYDREAMER,' says Mrs Dawson.

Mrs Dawson is my Year 2 teacher. She invites my mother to come in for a chat.

A serious chat.

About my daydreaming.

I'm good at distracting Mum

from bad things my teacher

says. I fake a dizzy turn.

I knock three books, an apple and the goldfish bowl off Mrs Dawson's desk.

Mum freaks out. Which proves that I'm also good at acting.

'You are an exceptional actor, Lottie Perkins,' I say to myself. 'You should be a MOVIE STAR!'

CHAPTER 2

'I'm going to be a movie star!' I tell my pet goat, Feta.

'BAA!' says Feta. That's goat talk for, 'About time, Lottie. You have real talent.'

'I'm going to be a movie star!' I tell

Mum.

'Stop shouting, Charlotte Emily

Perkins!' she snaps.

Mum always calls me Charlotte

Emily Perkins when she's cross.

Like last night …

'Come here at once, Charlotte Emily Perkins!'

And last Sunday …

'What on EARTH have you done to your grandmother's wallpaper, Charlotte Emily Perkins?'

And last Christmas …

'Did *you* bring that stray donkey home, Charlotte Emily Perkins?'

'I'm going to be a movie star!'

I tell my class.

'Don't be a PEA BRAIN,' says

Harper Dark. 'You couldn't be

a movie star in a million years.'

So rude! And nasty!

But that's Harper Dark for you.

She's a bully and my arch-enemy.

I'm good at ignoring Harper Dark. Most of the time.

'I'm going to be a movie star!' I tell my best friend, Sam Bell.

'Really?' shouts Sam. 'Well, pickle my pants! What a great idea!'

And *that's* why Sam is my best friend. He's kind and funny and smart and says crazy things like, 'Pickle my pants!'

And he believes in me.

CHAPTER 3

'LIGHTS! CAMERA! ACTION!'

yells Sam.

Sam films Feta eating my

homework. He films it all the way

through.

'Why didn't you stop her?' I ask.

Sam shrugs. 'The light on her

horns was so pretty. And I couldn't find the stop button on the video camera.'

Never mind. No homework means more time to choose my movie-star costume.

'LIGHTS! CAMERA! ACTION!'

yells Sam.

Sam films me as I walk across
the living room. I'm wearing
Mum's best dress. It's red with
sparkles around the hem. It's short
on Mum, but comes down to the
floor on me. My shoes, pearls,
gloves and fur wrap are from the
dress-up box.

'You look fabulous, Lottie!' cries
Sam. 'Like a real movie star.'

'Thanks,' I say.

I flash my best movie-star smile at the camera and keep walking.

I trip over the dress and fall flat on my face.

'LIGHTS! CAMERA! ACTION!' yells Sam.

Sam films me the next day at school. I'm eating an egg sandwich.

I bite into the bread as though I'm angry.

I chew like I'm deep in thought.

I wipe the crumbs off my face

like I'm scared.

'Butter my boots!' cries Sam.

'You are a SUPER-DUPER actor!'

CHAPTER 4

'You are a HOPELESS actor!' shouts Harper Dark.

Harper stands before me with her hands on her hips. Jane Chang and Eve Roberts stand behind her. They all smirk.

Harper Dark is good at getting other girls to be mean. But I don't know why she bothers. She's mean enough all on her own.

'You'll never be a movie star,' says Harper. 'Movie stars don't scream and holler when they play dodgeball. They don't skin their knees. They don't eat smelly egg sandwiches. And they don't have stupid-head names like POTTIE LERKINS.'

I glare at Harper Dark,

but inside I'm feeling small and
ugly. Bullies do that to you.

'Her name is Lottie Perkins,'
whispers Sam. 'And filming starts
tomorrow, so she really *will* be
a movie star.'

Sam blushes at his own bravery.

Harper narrows her eyes.

'What's the movie about?'
she asks.

I stare at Sam.

Sam stares at me.

'You have no idea, do you?'
asks Harper.

We have no idea. Absolutely no
idea. But we cannot tell Harper
Dark that.

'It's an ADVENTURE movie!'
I shout.

'With pirates and sea monsters!'
yells Sam.

'And there's a love story too,'
I say.

'With funny bits,' adds Sam.

'And sad bits,' I say. 'People like
crying at the movies.'

'And scary battles with sword fights and explosions and aliens!' shouts Sam.

I chew on my lip. I hope we haven't gone too far.

'It sounds stupid,' snorts Harper.

She stomps away. Jane and Eve follow.

'Rattle my ribs!' gasps Sam. 'I think it sounds GREAT!'

Me too!

CHAPTER 5

This is it! We're filming a real movie. And I'm the STAR!

Mum's garden shed has been turned into a café. My rabbits sit around a plate, eating grass. I've dressed them as Mary Poppins, Queen Elizabeth and

Captain Hook. This is the sort of café where famous people come to eat and fight and fall in love and set out on adventures with pirates.

I'm wearing Mum's red dress again, plus the fur wrap, pearls, gloves and high-heeled shoes.

Feta is wearing Dad's shirt, tie and underpants.

'Take care,' I tell Feta. 'That tie is silk. Very expensive. Mum bought it in Paris. She'll be mad if anything happens to it. Crazy mad.'

'LIGHTS! CAMERA! ACTION!'

yells Sam.

Feta and I gaze at each other
across the table.

I chew a piece of toast into
a heart shape.

I reach out and grab Feta's hoof in my hand.

'Harold,' I sigh. 'I think I'm in love.'

'BAA!' says Feta. That's goat talk for, 'I love you too, my darling.'

I flutter my eyelashes and that's when I see her!

Harper Dark.

Peering through the shed window.

Smirking.

'Juggle a duck!' shouts Sam. 'What's she doing here?'

I dash to the window and breathe heavily. It fogs up. I write backwards: GO AWAY!

'That's sorted!' I shout. 'Back to filming!'

But when I turn around, a terrible sight meets my eyes. The rabbits have gobbled all the grass and filled their plate

with poop. Even worse, Feta has
eaten her underpants and is now
nibbling on her tie.

'No, Feta!' I scream. 'STOP!'

Feta bolts from the shed.

CHAPTER 6

I chase Feta into the garden.

Harper Dark steps out from behind a rose bush.

'Shut the gate!' I shout.

Harper smirks and holds the gate WIDE OPEN with her foot.

Feta bounces out onto the footpath, chewing the tie as she goes.

I dash after her, but trip on the hem of my dress. Mum's best red dress. I hear something tear. I fall and my knees sting.

I scramble to my feet. Now I'm *really* upset. I'm cross with Harper. I'm mad at Feta. And my hair and clothes are a mess.

'BAA!' Feta trots away down the middle of the street. 'Chomp! Chomp! Burp!'

I chase Feta around the corner
and run straight into a crowd of
people.

'Help! Help! Get out of my way!'
I'm screaming and rolling my eyes
and waving my arms in the air and
pushing and shoving like a maniac.

'CUT!' cries a deep, loud voice.

The crowd freezes. Everything falls silent.

Whoops!

I've run right into the middle of a real live movie set.

'Marvellous!'

A man wearing a black beret
waddles towards me.

'Your scream is truly marvellous!'
he shouts. 'And your clothes and

hair are a mess. A MARVELLOUS mess!'

'Thanks,' I say. 'I'm Lottie Perkins. I'm an exceptional child.'

'Indeed,' the man agrees. 'I'm Bo Bloom. I'm a famous movie director.'

CHAPTER 7

Bo is making a movie about a giant gorilla. Today he's filming a scene where the gorilla chases people through the city. He wants me to be at the front of the crowd!

'ME?' I gasp. 'In your big movie?'

Bo nods.

Harper Dark pops out from behind a camera man. She's been spying on me. AGAIN!

'What about me?' asks Harper in a sweet voice. She smiles and smooths her perfect hair.

Bo stares at Harper. He rubs his chin.

'Sorry,' says Bo. 'You look far too tidy to have been chased by a giant gorilla.'

And your voice is too soft.

Too sweet. We need raw terror.

Loud screams. Hollering.'

Harper kicks Bo in the shins and

storms off.

Just then, Sam squeezes through

the crowd. I whisper something in

Bo's ear and he nods. He plonks
Sam in the director's chair and
hands him a loudspeaker.

'LIGHTS! CAMERA! ACTION!'
yells Sam.

I'm being chased by a giant gorilla.

'Help! Help! Get out of my way!' I'm screaming and rolling my eyes and waving my arms in the air and pushing and shoving like a maniac. I make my way to the front of the crowd and find myself staring right into the camera lens.

'CUT!' cries Bo.

'Perfect!' shouts Sam.

Feta trots over. A clump of gorilla fur is hanging from her mouth.

'BAA!' she says. That's goat talk for, 'Sorry about the tie, but all's well that ends well.'

CHAPTER 8

Sam and I are at the movies.

We've just watched Bo Bloom's

latest film, *Gorilla Fear*.

'Pickle my pants!' cries

Sam. 'That was brilliant!

Terrifying! Thrilling!

And your running and
screaming and arm-waving
were the best by far, Lottie.'

The credits roll and my name
comes onto the screen.

'LOOK! LOOK!' I shout.
'I'm listed as an extra.'

'Extra?' asks Sam.

'Extra actor,' I explain.

Harper Dark is sitting three rows
in front of us. She turns back and
stares daggers.

'Extra jealous,' I whisper.

'Don't worry about her,' says Sam. 'You're the REAL extra.'

'You're right!' I shout. 'I'm extra special! Extra talented! Extra happy! Extra excited to be famous!'

Suddenly, I notice that everyone in the cinema is staring at me. I giggle, then flash them my best smile. My extra-bright movie-star smile.

THE END

Look like a MOVIE STAR.
Choose at least four of these
things to wear or hold:

💜 sunglasses
💜 a sparkly red dress
💜 high heels
💜 long gloves
💜 an enormous bunch of flowers
💜 a fur shawl
💜 a feather boa
💜 a pearl necklace
💜 diamond earrings
💜 bright red lipstick
💜 a pen for signing autographs
💜 a fancy handbag
💜 a tiny, fluffy white dog
💜 a tiny, fluffy white dog in
   a fancy handbag

COLLECT THEM ALL!

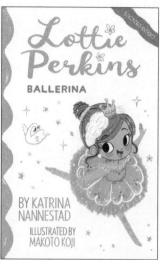